The City We Found

Mrigendra Bharti

Published by Sellbrochure Vymish Entertainment, 2024.

This is a work of fiction. Similarities to real people, places, or events are entirely coincidental.

THE CITY WE FOUND

First edition. June 25, 2024.

Copyright © 2024 Mrigendra Bharti.

ISBN: 979-8224850471

Written by Mrigendra Bharti.

Table of Contents

Preface

The city never sleeps, they say. And neither did the idea for this book. It sprouted, like a tenacious weed pushing through concrete cracks, during a seemingly ordinary weekend trip. Little did I know, that stolen sunrise on a rooftop, shared with a newfound friend, would ignite a creative spark that would illuminate a whole new world.

"The City We Found" isn't just a story about art, though art plays a vital role. It's a story about connection, about finding beauty in the unexpected, and about the transformative power of seeing the world through a different lens. It's a love letter to the city, a place that can be both intimidating and exhilarating, a place where anonymity can breed loneliness, but where shared experiences can forge unbreakable bonds.

Arjun, the protagonist, embodies the initial apprehension many of us feel when faced with the urban sprawl. He's an artist with a comfort zone, hesitant to embrace the chaos of city life. Riya, with her infectious enthusiasm and rebellious streak, becomes his guide, his muse, and his partner in artistic exploration. Together, they navigate the city's labyrinthine streets, discovering hidden gems and uncovering stories waiting to be captured on canvas.

Their journey mirrors my own experiences, of finding inspiration in the most unexpected places. Stolen moments on rooftops, conversations with fellow artists in bustling cafes, and the quiet contemplation of cityscapes bathed in the golden hues of dawn – these experiences became the seeds of this story.

Within these pages, you'll find a celebration of artistic expression, a testament to the power of shared passions, and a love story that blooms amidst the neon glow of the cityscape. So, grab a cup of coffee, settle in for a read, and prepare to be swept away on a journey of artistic exploration, where a single sunrise can change everything.

Let "The City We Found" be an invitation to see your own city with fresh eyes, to find beauty in the ordinary, and to embrace the unexpected connections that await you around every corner. Happy reading!

Prologue

The wind whipped around Arjun's face, carrying with it the scent of exhaust fumes and something faintly floral. He clutched his sketchbook tighter, its worn leather cover offering little comfort against the biting November chill. Below him, the city sprawled out like a concrete ocean – a sea of towering buildings, their windows aglow like fireflies trapped in a steel cage.

He wasn't supposed to be here. Not on this rooftop, not in this city. He was a creature of habit, of quaint cafes and well-worn paths. The city, with its cacophony of honking horns and ceaseless movement, had always felt overwhelming. Yet, here he was, perched precariously on the edge of a world he barely knew, drawn by an impulsive invitation and a promise of a sunrise unlike any other.

Across from him stood Riya, a whirlwind of energy wrapped in a red leather jacket. Her hair, a shock of blue under the pale moon, danced in the wind as she pointed at the eastern horizon. "See that faint light? That's where the magic begins, sunrise artist."

Arjun squinted, trying to pierce the veil of darkness, a mix of apprehension and anticipation bubbling in his chest. "Are you sure about this?" he asked, his voice barely audible over the city's low hum.

Riya's smile was infectious. "Trust me," she said, her voice laced with an excitement that was both contagious and terrifying. "This city, this sunrise, it'll change the way you see everything."

Her words hung in the air, a promise shrouded in the mysteries of the night. Arjun wasn't sure if he believed her, but as the faintest hint of pink crept onto the horizon, painting the edges of the buildings in a soft glow, he couldn't help but be drawn in. This was more than a stolen sunrise; it was a chance to see the city with new eyes, a chance for an adventure he never expected, a chance for something unexpected to bloom in the heart of the concrete jungle. He flipped open his sketchbook, his fingers hovering over the blank page, ready to capture the magic that Riya promised, the magic that might just change his whole world.

Acknowledgments

This book is a testament to the power of unexpected encounters, the kind that leave an indelible mark on your soul. It's a love letter to the city, not just for its towering structures and bustling streets, but for the hidden beauty waiting to be discovered in stolen moments and shared experiences.

A special thank you goes out to the city itself, for its relentless energy and the stories it whispers in the wind. Gratitude also to the countless artists, both known and unknown, whose passion and creativity fueled my own.

Finally, to the muse who sparked the initial flame – your infectious enthusiasm and belief in the magic of a city sunrise will forever be etched in my memory.

Thank you for being a part of this journey, even if it was just for a single, unforgettable sunrise.

Introduction

The city, a tapestry woven from steel and glass, stretched out before Arjun, a million fireflies awakening against the twilight canvas. The fiery hues of the sunset bled into a gentle lavender, and a crescent moon peeked through the inky blackness, casting a silvery glow on the buildings below. Yet, for Arjun, the cityscape felt curiously lifeless. He was a landscape artist, a master of capturing the soul of a place in a brushstroke, but here, amidst the urban sprawl, inspiration eluded him.

A gentle nudge from beside him broke his reverie. "Ready to paint the symphony, sunrise artist?" Riya's voice was a soft whisper woven into the cool night air.

Arjun turned to her, the city lights reflected in her eyes. A hint of a smile played on his lips. "More than ever," he replied, a newfound determination replacing his initial apprehension. This wasn't just about capturing a sunrise; it was about capturing a new beginning, a shared experience on a canvas far larger than anything he'd ever imagined.

He uncapped his pen, the scratch against the paper a counterpoint to the city's low hum. His initial strokes were bold, capturing the city's structure, the relentless energy that pulsed through its veins. But something was missing. The sketch, though technically sound, lacked the vibrancy, the stories that thrummed beneath the city's surface.

"What's wrong?" Riya asked, her voice laced with concern as she leaned closer.

Arjun sighed, frustration gnawing at him. "I can't seem to capture it," he confessed, gesturing towards the glittering cityscape. "It feels... lifeless."

Riya smiled, a knowing glint in her eyes. "Maybe you're looking at the city the wrong way," she suggested. "It's not just steel and glass, Arjun. It's a living, breathing entity – a canvas of stories waiting to be told."

Her words struck a chord. He closed his eyes, trying to see the cityscape through her eyes. He imagined the artists in their studios, pouring their souls onto canvases. He heard the rhythmic hum of traffic, not as noise, but as a symphony of purposeful movement. He saw the quiet moments – a couple sharing a romantic kiss on a rooftop bar, a window glowing with the warm light of a home.

When he opened his eyes, the city had transformed. He saw the beauty not just in the architecture, but in the stories it held. He saw the vibrant energy of the city, the relentless spirit that never slept.

He picked up his pen once more, this time with renewed purpose. His strokes became more deliberate, capturing the essence of the city's soul. He used vibrant colors to represent the energy, muted tones for the quiet moments, and swirling lines to depict the constant movement. With each stroke, the city on his canvas came alive. It was no longer a static landscape, but a vibrant tapestry of stories, emotions, and experiences.

As the last stars surrendered to the encroaching dawn, a sense of satisfaction coursed through him. He had captured not just a place, but a feeling, a connection that transcended the boundaries of their different worlds. He looked at Riya, eager to share his creation. "What do you think?"

Riya's eyes widened in surprise, a smile blossoming on her face. "Wow, Arjun," she breathed. "It's... it's incredible. You captured the heart of the city, the stories, the soul."

Arjun felt a warmth spread through him, a validation of his artistic vision. This wasn't just a painting; it was a bridge between his world and Riya's. It was a way for him to express the newfound love he felt for the city, a love that began with her.

About Sellbrochure Vymish Entertainment

Sellbrochure Vymish Entertainment, recognized as India's largest book publishing company, has made significant strides in ensuring its extensive collection of books reaches audiences across the global market. This rapid expansion is a testament to the company's dedication to disseminating knowledge and literature far beyond national borders. Central to its success is its affiliation with InkWhirl Media Networks, a reputable entity in the media and publication industry known for its innovative and strategic approaches. Within this network, InkWhirl Publication LLC operates as a vital division, further enhancing the company's capabilities and reach in the international market.

The visionary behind this enterprise is Mrigendra Bharti, the founder of Sellbrochure Vymish Entertainment. His foresight and passion for the literary world have been instrumental in steering the company towards remarkable growth and recognition. Under his leadership, Sellbrochure Vymish Entertainment has not only expanded its catalog but also established a strong presence in both domestic and international markets. Mrigendra Bharti's commitment to excellence and innovation has been a driving force in the company's journey, ensuring that it stays ahead of industry trends and meets the evolving needs of readers worldwide.

Sellbrochure Vymish Entertainment operates under the robust support of its parental organization, Mrigendra Bharti Group InfoTech. This affiliation provides the necessary resources and strategic guidance, enabling the publishing company to undertake ambitious projects and explore new markets. Mrigendra Bharti Group InfoTech's extensive experience in technology and information services has been a valuable asset, allowing Sellbrochure Vymish Entertainment to integrate advanced digital solutions in its operations, thereby enhancing its distribution capabilities and reader engagement.

Through relentless efforts and a commitment to quality, Sellbrochure Vymish Entertainment continues to break barriers and expand the reach of Indian literature globally. The company's diverse portfolio includes a wide range of genres, catering to different age groups and interests, thereby fostering a rich and inclusive reading culture. As it continues to innovate and grow, Sellbrochure Vymish Entertainment remains dedicated to its mission of making literature accessible to all, contributing significantly to the global literary landscape.

Connect With Mrigendra,
Thank you very much for choosing this book.
You can also connect with me on Instagram,
https://www.instagram.com/i_mrigendrabharti.official
With Love,
Mrigendra Bharti

Chapter 1: A Brush with Destiny

The scent of drying oil paints hung heavy in the air, a familiar comfort that wrapped around Arjun like a well-worn sweater. Sunlight streamed through the attic window, illuminating the dust motes dancing in its golden rays. He squinted at his latest canvas, a vibrant dance of colors depicting a sunrise over his hometown's rolling wheat fields. Each brushstroke held a memory - the fiery kiss of the dawn on his skin as he perched on the old oak tree behind his house, the way the wind rustled through the wheat, creating a symphony that only his ears could hear, the damp coolness of the grass beneath his bare feet as he chased fireflies in the twilight. Arjun wasn't just painting a landscape; he was painting a feeling, a tapestry of emotions woven from the threads of his life in this small, sun-drenched corner of the world.

Arjun, a creature of habit as steady as the grandfather clock downstairs in the bakery, rarely ventured far from his studio. The rhythmic clatter of his grandmother kneading dough and the yeasty aroma that permeated the house were the comforting constants in his life. His days unfolded with the predictable grace of a well-rehearsed ballet. He'd wake up before dawn, lured out of bed by the first blush of pink in the eastern sky. A steaming mug of his grandmother's special chai, brewed with a secret blend of spices passed down through generations, would be his companion as he climbed the creaky stairs to his attic haven. There, bathed in the golden light of sunrise, he'd lose himself in his art. The world outside, with its relentless demands and hurried pace, would fade away, replaced by the vibrant world he created on canvas. He'd meticulously clean his brushes, each stroke a ritualistic cleansing, preparing them to dance across the canvas, leaving behind their colorful footprints. The selection of pigments was a ceremony in itself, a careful consideration of hues and tones, ensuring they captured the essence of the scene he envisioned. Finally, with a deep breath and a silent prayer whispered to the muse that guided his hand, he'd approach the blank canvas. It was an intimidating expanse of white at first, a vast emptiness waiting to be filled. But as the first brushstroke touched the surface, a spark would ignite, and the canvas would slowly transform, blossoming with life under his touch.

He thrived in the solitude of his attic studio. The silence, broken only by the gentle scrape of brush against canvas and the rhythmic chirping of sparrows outside his window, was his muse. The world outside, with its relentless noise and the whirlwind of human interactions, felt overwhelming and foreign. He was content with the company of his paints, their vibrant hues a language he understood better than any spoken word.

But today, a rare invitation had disrupted his peaceful routine. A prestigious art exhibition in the bustling city, a place that seemed as foreign to him as the moon, had extended a slender thread of opportunity, pulling him out of his cozy cocoon. The news arrived tucked away in a crisp envelope addressed in elegant calligraphy, a stark contrast to the worn stationery he usually received. Inside, the words danced on the page, an official invitation to showcase his art at the renowned City Art Gallery. A tremor of excitement, laced with a healthy dose of apprehension, ran through him. The city, a place he only knew from the grainy black and white photographs in his grandfather's old travelogues, was an overwhelming assault on his senses. Towering buildings scraped the sky, their steel and glass facades reflecting the harsh sunlight in a way that made his eyes ache. The air, thick with exhaust fumes and the cacophony of car horns, felt heavy on his lungs, a stark contrast to the crisp, wheat-scented air of his hometown. Navigating the crowded streets, he felt like a lone sunflower lost in a concrete jungle, his worn leather satchel bumping awkwardly against his hip.

Reaching the grand exhibition hall, its imposing marble facade dwarfing him, Arjun fumbled with the worn leather satchel, the once-crisp invitation peeking out like a nervous smile. The weight of it felt foreign in his hand, a contrast to the familiar comfort of his paintbrushes. Taking a deep breath, he pushed open the heavy oak doors. The scent of oil paint, usually a source of solace, was now mixed with the metallic tang of cleaning supplies and a faint undercurrent of expensive perfume. Inside, a kaleidoscope of colors and textures bombarded him. Abstract sculptures jutted out from pedestals like misshapen giants, their forms defying interpretation. Photorealistic portraits hung on stark white walls, capturing every wrinkle and imperfection with a ruthless honesty that made him squirm. Arjun, ever the observer, felt a pang of self-doubt. His art, rooted in pastoral simplicity, the soft hues and gentle brushstrokes reflecting the quiet beauty of his world, seemed

...to belong in a quaint farmhouse kitchen, not amidst this gallery of bold statements and jarring juxtapositions. He retreated to a quiet corner, his heart hammering a nervous rhythm against his ribs, a rhythm that had nothing to do with the art around him and everything to do with the unfamiliar world he'd stepped into.

The confident strides he'd taken through the bustling city streets seemed a distant memory now. Here, surrounded by these intimidating artworks and the hushed murmurs of art critics and socialites, he felt like a small-town boy who'd wandered into a grand ballroom. Self-consciousness tightened its grip on him, making his worn clothes and paint-stained fingers feel like glaring accusations. He longed for the familiar comfort of his studio, the worn wooden easel, and the reassuring scent of his paints.

A movement in his peripheral vision caught his eye. A young woman, her fiery red hair a stark contrast to the muted tones of the gallery, stood transfixed before a particularly abstract piece. Her brow was furrowed in concentration, her lips moving silently as if she were having a conversation with the artwork itself. Intrigued, Arjun stole a closer look. She was dressed in a stylish pantsuit, the tailored lines belying a hint of artistic flair in the way the scarf around her neck was knotted in a nonchalant but deliberate way. As she moved on to another piece, her eyes sparkling with curiosity, Arjun found himself drawn to her. There was an energy about her, a vibrancy that mirrored the colors in the paintings she admired.

Hesitantly, Arjun took a step closer, drawn by an invisible force. He cleared his throat, the sound echoing awkwardly in the hushed gallery. The woman turned, her emerald eyes widening in surprise for a moment before a warm smile spread across her face.

"Excuse me," Arjun stammered, the words catching in his throat. "I... I couldn't help but notice your interest in that piece."

He gestured awkwardly towards the abstract sculpture she'd been studying moments ago.

"Oh!" she replied, her voice a delightful mix of amusement and surprise. "I wouldn't say interest exactly. More like confusion," she admitted with a laugh that tinkled like wind chimes. "It's fascinating, but I can't quite grasp what the artist is trying to convey."

Arjun felt a flicker of relief. He wasn't the only one who found some of these pieces challenging. Taking a deep breath, he ventured, "Well, sometimes abstract art is open to interpretation. What do you see?"

Her eyes widened again, this time with genuine interest. "Hmm," she mused, tilting her head to one side as she contemplated the sculpture. "I see... a struggle. A jumbled mess of emotions trying to find a form." She turned to Arjun, a question dancing in her eyes. "What do you see?"

Arjun hesitated, surprised by the invitation. He wasn't used to discussing his art with strangers, but something about this woman, her openness and genuine curiosity, disarmed him. "I see... growth," he admitted softly. "The chaos is necessary, I think. It's the breaking down of old structures to make way for something new."

A slow smile spread across her face. "That's a beautiful interpretation," she said, her voice filled with warmth. "I never thought of it that way."

They fell into conversation, a hesitant dance at first, then flowing more easily as they discovered a shared passion for art, albeit expressed in vastly different ways. She, Riya, was an art critic, her sharp mind dissecting the technical aspects of each piece, while he, Arjun, approached art with an emotional connection, seeking the stories hidden beneath the surface. Their contrasting perspectives sparked a lively debate, each challenging the other's way of seeing the world.

As the afternoon wore on, the initial awkwardness melted away, replaced by a sense of comfortable companionship. They wandered through the gallery, stopping to discuss various artworks, their voices weaving a tapestry of observation and interpretation. Arjun, usually so reserved, found himself captivated by Riya's energy and her infectious enthusiasm. He learned about her fast-paced life in the city, a world away from his quiet hometown, and she, in turn, listened intently as he spoke about his art, his voice gaining confidence with each passing moment.

The setting sun cast long shadows across the gallery floor as the announcement for the closing of the exhibition echoed through the halls. Arjun felt a pang of disappointment. He had been so engrossed in their conversation that he'd lost track of time.

"Well," Riya said with a sigh, "it seems our time here is up. But this was delightful, Arjun. Thank

"...you for the conversation. It's rare to meet someone who can see art in such a unique way."

Arjun, his cheeks flushing a warm red, stammered, "T-thank you too. I, uh, I enjoyed talking to you as well."

An awkward silence descended between them, punctuated only by the distant murmur of departing guests. Arjun desperately wanted to ask her out, to extend this unexpected connection beyond the confines of the gallery walls. But the words wouldn't come. His usual eloquence in the language of art deserted him when it came to the language of love.

Riya, sensing his hesitation, broke the silence with a playful smile. "So, tell me, Arjun, the artist behind the sunrise masterpiece," she gestured towards a painting displayed across the hall, the vibrant hues catching the last rays of sunlight, "where can I find more of your work?"

Relief washed over him. This was his chance. He quickly retrieved his worn business card, a simple affair with his name and a picture of his studio etched on it, from his satchel and handed it to her.

"This has my contact information," he explained, his voice gaining a hint of confidence. "I, uh, I also have a website where I showcase some of my paintings."

Riya took the card, her eyes scanning the details. A mischievous glint sparked in them. "Well, Arjun, the sunrise artist," she said, her voice laced with a playful challenge, "consider this an invitation to a private exhibition. Let's see if your art can impress a city critic in her natural habitat."

Before Arjun could stammer a reply, she extended her hand, her smile radiating warmth. "It was a pleasure meeting you, Arjun. I look forward to seeing more of your work."

With a final wink, she turned and disappeared into the throng of exiting patrons, leaving Arjun standing there, his heart pounding a frantic rhythm against his ribs. He clutched the business card in his hand, a small, worn piece of paper that now felt like a lifeline to a future he couldn't have imagined just hours ago. The invitation to the art exhibition had propelled him out of his comfort zone, but this unexpected encounter with Riya had thrown his entire world into delightful disarray. A nervous smile spread across his face as he realized that stepping outside his routine might just be the most beautiful stroke of fate his life had ever seen.

The rusty bell above the bakery door chimed a cheerful melody as Riya stepped inside. The warm aroma of freshly baked bread washed over her, mingling with the faint scent of oil paint that seemed to waft from somewhere above. A wave of nostalgia hit her as she looked around the familiar bakery, its décor unchanged since her childhood visits. Her grandfather, Arjun's, had been a regular customer, and she'd often accompanied him, her nose buried in a sketchbook while he indulged in the bakery's famous cinnamon rolls.

A young woman with flour-dusted hands emerged from behind the counter, a warm smile lighting up her face as she recognized Riya. "Riya! It's so good to see you again," she exclaimed, wiping her hands on her apron. "Come, come, let me introduce you to someone."

She led Riya up the creaky stairs, her stories about Arjun tumbling out in a rapid-fire stream. Riya learned about his quiet ways, his love for art, and how he spent most of his days locked away in his attic studio. By the time they reached the top of the stairs, Riya felt a strange mix of excitement and nervousness.

The studio door stood ajar, a sliver of sunlight illuminating the worn wooden floorboards. Riya peeked inside, her breath catching in her throat. Sunlight streamed through the attic window, casting a warm glow over the room. Canvases of varying sizes leaned against the walls, each one a vibrant tapestry of colors and emotions. In the center of the room, an easel stood proudly, displaying a new untitled painting. But what truly captured Riya's attention was the man standing beside it, a shy smile playing on his lips.

"Arjun," Riya said, her voice barely a whisper.

He turned, his eyes widening in surprise before a smile bloomed on his face, brighter than the colors on his latest creation. "Riya! You came," he said, his voice slightly choked with emotion.

"Of course I came," she replied, stepping into the room. As she moved closer to the paintings, each one unfolded a story, a glimpse into Arjun's world. There were landscapes bathed in the golden light of dawn, portraits that captured the essence of his small-town life, and even a few abstract pieces that hinted at a hidden depth to his artistic soul.

"They're amazing," Riya finally said, her voice filled with genuine admiration. "Each one tells a story, evokes an emotion."

Arjun's cheeks flushed a faint pink. "Thank you," he mumbled, shuffling his feet awkwardly. "I, uh, I took your advice to heart. Tried to express myself a little differently."

Their conversation flowed easily this time, as if picking up right where they left off at the gallery. Riya pointed out details in his paintings, sparking discussions about his inspiration and artistic process. He, in turn, asked about her life in the city, a world he still viewed with a mixture of fascination and trepidation.

As they talked, Riya noticed a change in Arjun. The shy boy from the gallery seemed to have faded into the background, replaced by a man with a newfound confidence, his eyes sparkling with passion as he spoke about his art. The city muse had unknowingly awakened the artist within.

Hours melted away as they delved deeper into each other's worlds. The warm aroma of freshly baked bread wafted up from the bakery below, a reminder of the time.

"Oh my goodness," Riya exclaimed, looking at the clock on the wall. "I completely lost track of time. I'm so sorry."

Arjun chuckled softly. "Don't worry about it. I'm glad you could stay."

There was a comfortable silence between them, a silent question hanging in the air. Arjun gathered his courage and spoke. "Riya, I was wondering..." he stammered, his voice trailing off.

"Yes?" she prompted, her eyes filled with curiosity.

"Would you like to see a real sunrise sometime?" he asked, his voice barely above a whisper. "Maybe even paint it?"

A slow smile spread across Riya's face. "I'd like that very much," she said, her voice filled with warmth. "But only if you promise to show me the secrets of the sunrise artist's world."

Arjun's smile mirrored hers. "Deal," he replied, extending his hand towards her.

As she placed her hand in his, a warmth spread through him, dispelling the last remnants of his shyness. He had stepped outside his comfort zone, and in doing so, had found not just inspiration for his art, but a connection that promised to paint his life

Chapter 2: Brushstrokes of Dawn

The first blush of pink peeked over the horizon, painting the eastern sky in hues of coral and lavender. A gentle breeze, carrying the sweet scent of wildflowers, rustled through the wheat fields, creating a symphony that only Arjun could hear. He stood perched on the familiar oak tree behind his house, a worn backpack slung over his shoulder, a weathered easel propped against the gnarled trunk. Today wasn't just any sunrise; it was a sunrise painted with the promise of something new. Today, Riya would be joining him.

The days leading up to this moment had been filled with a nervous anticipation that danced between excitement and trepidation. Arjun hadn't ventured beyond the sunrise with anyone, not even his family. It was his time, his moment of solitary communion with nature that fueled his art. But the thought of sharing this special ritual with Riya, the city muse who had awakened a vibrant energy within him, outweighed his initial reservations.

He'd woken up before dawn, his usually calm sleep disturbed by dreams of bustling city streets and vibrant art galleries, all punctuated by glimpses of Riya's fiery red hair and the emerald depths of her eyes. He wasn't sure what to expect from her reaction to his world, so different from the one she inhabited. But the desire to bridge the gap between them, to share a piece of soul with her, was stronger than any fear.

As the light grew stronger, casting long shadows across the fields, Arjun heard a familiar rustle in the bushes below. He craned his neck and saw Riya emerge, her hair a fiery halo against the rising sun. She was dressed in jeans and a comfortable sweater, a stark contrast to the sleek pantsuit she'd worn at the gallery. But even in casual attire, she carried herself with an air of effortless grace.

"Wow," she breathed, her eyes widening as she took in the breathtaking vista before her. The rolling wheat fields stretched out like a golden sea, dotted with wildflowers like colorful jewels. In the distance, a meandering river shimmered like a silver ribbon.

Arjun smiled, his anxieties melting away in the warmth of her appreciation. "Welcome to my sunrise," he said, his voice filled with a quiet pride.

Riya walked towards him, her eyes sparkling with curiosity. "It's... perfect," she said, her voice soft. "So peaceful, so serene. It's hard to believe such a bustling city exists just a few hours away."

Arjun helped her climb the sturdy branches of the oak tree, their positions creating a comfortable closeness. He pointed out familiar landmarks: the old church steeple peeking through the trees in the distance, the small farmhouse where his childhood friend lived, the winding path he often took for his morning jogs. Riya listened intently, absorbing his world like a thirsty sponge.

As the sun climbed higher, casting its golden rays upon their faces, a comfortable silence descended. Arjun watched Riya, mesmerized by the way the sunlight danced in her hair and cast a warm glow on her face. He understood now why he'd been so captivated by her at the art exhibition. She exuded not just beauty, but a vibrant energy that seemed to reflect the colors of his paintings.

He cleared his throat, breaking the silence. "You know," he said hesitantly, "I wasn't sure you'd come."

Riya turned towards him, a playful smile tugging at the corners of her lips. "Why wouldn't I?" she countered. "You offered a glimpse into your world, a piece of your soul. And honestly, who turns down the chance to witness a real sunrise with the sunrise artist himself?"

Arjun felt a warmth bloom in his chest. "I wouldn't want anyone else to see it for the first time," he admitted, his voice barely above a whisper.

The words hung in the air, charged with unspoken meaning. Riya's gaze lingered on his face for a moment before she turned to the landscape, her expression thoughtful.

"Tell me, Arjun," she said, her voice breaking the fragile tension, "what inspires you in a sunrise?"

Arjun pondered the question, his eyes taking in the vast panorama before him. "It's not just the beauty," he finally explained. "It's the promise of a new beginning. Every sunrise wipes the slate clean, gives you a chance to start fresh. It's that sense of hope, of possibility, that I try to capture in my paintings."

Riya nodded, a flicker of understanding passing through her eyes. "That makes sense," she said. "I suppose that's why your art resonates with me. It's more than just colors and textures; it's about the emotions you evoke."

They fell into conversation, a comfortable

conversation that flowed as effortlessly as the rising sun. Riya talked about her life in the city, a whirlwind of deadlines, art openings, and critiques. Arjun listened intently, captivated by her world, so different from his own. He learned about the pressure to constantly analyze and dissect art, to find hidden meanings and underlying social commentary.

"It can be exhausting," Riya confessed, a hint of weariness creeping into her voice. "Sometimes I miss the simplicity, the ability to appreciate art for its beauty alone."

Arjun smiled. "That's what I love about sunrises," he said. "There's no hidden meaning, no complex message. Just pure beauty and the promise of a new day."

As the sun climbed higher, casting long shadows across the landscape, they decided to capture the scene in their own ways. Riya pulled out a small sketchbook and a set of charcoal pencils, her movements swift and practiced. Arjun, his heart pounding with a newfound excitement, unpacked his paints and brushes.

He squeezed out vibrant colors onto his palette – warm yellows for the sun, soft pinks and oranges for the sky, and rich greens for the wheat fields. He started with broad, sweeping strokes, capturing the essence of the vastness before him. As he worked, he felt a connection to the scene that transcended words. He was no longer just painting a sunrise; he was painting a feeling, a shared experience with Riya.

Every now and then, he would steal a glance at her. Riya's charcoal danced across the page, capturing the intricate details of the wildflowers swaying in the breeze and the distant farmhouse bathed in the golden morning light. Her brow furrowed in concentration, but there was a hint of a smile playing on her lips.

They worked in comfortable silence, the only sounds the rustling of leaves and the occasional chirping of birds. The tension from earlier had melted away, replaced by a sense of easy companionship. Time seemed to lose its meaning as they were enveloped in their creative pursuits.

Finally, as the sun reached its zenith, casting a harsh midday light upon the landscape, they both put down their tools. Arjun looked at his canvas, a feeling of satisfaction washing over him. It wasn't a perfect representation of the sunrise, but it captured the essence of the moment - the beauty of nature, the shared experience with Riya, and the blossoming connection between them.

Riya, too, seemed pleased with her charcoal sketch. "It's not a typical critical analysis," she admitted with a playful smile. "But for once, I just wanted to capture the feeling."

Arjun grinned. "I think you did," he said, his gaze lingering on the sketch. He was particularly taken with the way she'd captured the light reflecting in Riya's own eyes, a spark of something new that mirrored his own burgeoning feelings.

They packed up their supplies, a shared sense of accomplishment hanging in the air. As they climbed down from the oak tree, Arjun extended his hand to help Riya. Their fingers brushed, sending a jolt of electricity through him. He looked into her eyes, the emerald depths mirroring his own unspoken emotions.

"Thank you, Arjun," Riya said, her voice soft. "For sharing this with me. It's... it's more than just a sunrise."

Arjun returned her gaze, his heart pounding in his chest. "For me too," he replied, his voice barely above a whisper. A new dawn had painted more than just the sky; it had painted a spark of hope in his heart, a promise of a future brighter than any sunrise he'd ever witnessed.

The following days unfolded with a newfound lightness for Arjun. The morning ritual of witnessing the sunrise no longer felt solitary. He carried the memory of Riya's fiery hair ablaze in the morning light, the way her eyes mirrored the vast expanse of the sky, and the warmth of her hand brushing his. He poured these emotions into his paintings, imbuing them with a vibrancy they hadn't possessed before.

One afternoon, while working on a new landscape inspired by their sunrise encounter, a knock on his studio door startled him. He wiped his paint-stained fingers on his overalls and hesitantly called out, "Come in!"

The door creaked open, revealing Riya's smiling face. She held a brown paper bag in her hand, the aroma of freshly baked bread wafting in from behind her.

"Surprise!" she exclaimed, stepping into the studio. "I brought you some peace offerings."

Arjun's heart skipped a beat. "Peace offerings?" he stammered, a blush creeping up his neck.

Riya laughed. "Well, technically, they're cinnamon rolls from your grandfather's bakery," she explained, handing him the bag. "But considering your aversion to harsh critiques, I figured a bribe might be a better way to approach this."

Arjun chuckled, taking the bag from her. The warmth of her hand lingered even through the paper. "Come in," he gestured, inviting her further into the room. "Harsh critiques, huh? What did I do this time?"

Riya walked around the studio, her eyes scanning his latest paintings. "Nothing terrible," she admitted with a teasing smile. "But I do have some... observations."

Arjun braced himself, expecting a dissection of his brushstrokes and color choices. But Riya's observations were different. She pointed out the subtle shift in his palette, the way the light seemed to dance across his landscapes with a newfound energy. She spoke of the emotions she felt when she looked at his paintings, a sense of hope, of a world waiting to be explored.

As she discussed his art, her eyes sparkled with a genuine interest that left Arjun breathless. They spent the afternoon lost in conversation, her critiques turning into insightful discussions about their artistic perspectives. She challenged him to push his boundaries, to experiment with new techniques, and to capture not just the beauty of the world, but the emotions it evoked.

When the sun began to dip below the horizon, casting long shadows across the studio, they reluctantly looked up from their conversation.

"I should probably get going," Riya said with a sigh. "But this was wonderful, Arjun. Thank you for letting me see your work."

Arjun walked her to the door, a newfound confidence blooming in his chest. "Thank you for coming," he replied, his voice firm. "And for... for seeing me, not just my art."

Riya met his gaze, her eyes filled with warmth. "I see you, Arjun," she said softly. "And I like what I see."

She leaned forward, a mischievous glint in her eyes, and brushed a quick kiss against his cheek. Before Arjun could react, she was out the door, leaving him standing there with a pounding heart and a smile that wouldn't fade.

That night, as he lay awake in bed, the image of Riya's fiery hair and the warmth of her kiss replayed in his mind. He wasn't sure what the future held, but this new connection, sparked by a shared sunrise, filled him with a sense of possibility he hadn't felt in years. He knew, deep down, that his life, like his art, was about to be painted in vibrant new colors.

The following weeks buzzed with a delightful energy for Arjun. He wasn't just painting sunrises anymore; he was painting emotions, capturing the lingering warmth of Riya's touch, the fire in her emerald eyes, and the hope that blossomed in his chest with every stolen glance.

One crisp autumn afternoon, as the leaves began to blaze with vibrant hues, Riya surprised him again with a visit. This time, she wasn't alone. A tall man with an air of quiet confidence stood beside her, a camera slung over his shoulder.

"Arjun, meet David," Riya said, a hint of nervousness in her voice. "He's a photographer I work with sometimes, and he was incredibly impressed by your paintings after I showed them to him."

David extended a hand, his smile warm and genuine. "The pleasure's all mine, Arjun," he said. "Riya hasn't stopped raving about your work. I couldn't wait to see it for myself."

Arjun, momentarily flustered, shook David's hand. He felt a pang of something akin to jealousy, quickly overshadowed by his curiosity. The idea of someone else seeing his art, especially through a photographer's lens, gave him a nervous thrill.

He invited them into his studio, the familiar space now brimming with a newfound energy. David carefully examined each painting, his eyes lingering on the subtle details, the shifts in light and shadow. He asked thoughtful questions about Arjun's inspirations and creative process.

As they talked, Arjun learned that David wasn't just a photographer; he was a storyteller. He captured not just landscapes and portraits, but the essence of a place, the emotions of a moment. Listening to him, Arjun felt a spark of inspiration ignite within him. Perhaps, his art wasn't just about capturing the beauty of his small town; it was about telling its stories, the stories of its people, their hopes, and dreams.

Later that day, David proposed an unexpected collaboration. He wanted to take photographs of Arjun's paintings amidst the very landscapes that inspired them. He envisioned capturing the way Arjun's art intertwined with the real world, blurring the lines between reality and imagination.

Arjun's heart pounded with excitement. The idea of his art being seen by a wider audience, of his small-town stories finding a voice beyond the confines of his studio, was thrilling. He readily agreed, a newfound confidence blooming within him.

The next few days were a whirlwind of activity. Arjun and David scoured the countryside, finding the perfect locations to showcase his paintings. David's camera clicked rhythmically as he captured the wheat fields bathed in golden light, the quaint bakery adorned with a peeling paint sign, the majestic oak tree standing sentinel on the hilltop.

As they worked, Riya acted as their guide and muse, her enthusiasm contagious. She helped them find hidden gems, quaint cafes, and local artists who readily offered their support. Arjun found himself drawn not just to the beauty of the landscape, but to the warmth of the community, the stories etched in the weathered faces of the townspeople.

One evening, as they sat by a crackling fire in a local pub, sharing stories and laughter, the realization dawned on Arjun. He wasn't just collaborating with David; he was creating a bond with Riya, a connection that went beyond shared artistic visions.

He saw a spark of understanding in her eyes, a reflection of his own feelings.

As the night deepened, David excused himself, a mischievous grin playing on his lips. Left alone with Riya, a comfortable silence descended. Arjun gathered his courage and spoke. "Riya," he began, his voice barely a whisper. "There's something I..."

"Me too," Riya interrupted, a soft smile gracing her lips. She leaned closer, her emerald eyes shimmering in the firelight. "You've shown me a world beyond the chaotic beauty of the city, Arjun. A world of peace, of hope, and... maybe a little bit of love."

Arjun's heart soared. He didn't need to say another word. He leaned in, and their lips met in a kiss that was as warm and comforting as the crackling fire beside them. It was a kiss that promised a future as vibrant and hopeful as the sunrise paintings that had brought them together.

Chapter 3: Brushstrokes in the City

The bustling energy of the city felt like a foreign language to Arjun as he stepped out of the train station. Honking taxis, flashing billboards, and a constant murmur of voices created a cacophony that overwhelmed him. He squinted in the bright sunlight, clutching his worn backpack tighter, a shield against the sensory assault. He was a man of wheat fields and sunrises, and this urban jungle was a world away from his comfort zone.

But he was here for a reason. He was here for Riya.

Their connection, forged under the golden light of sunrises and nurtured by shared artistic passion, had blossomed into something more. They'd stolen moments between phone calls, exchanged passionate letters filled with dreams and fears, and now, at Riya's urging, he was here. Here to spend a weekend with her, to experience her world, and perhaps, to paint a new chapter in their story.

Riya had described her apartment with excitement – a cozy studio overlooking a bustling park, a haven for creativity amidst the chaos. Arjun, however, found himself navigating a maze of towering buildings, the map clutched in his hand failing to calm his nerves. He felt like a misplaced brushstroke on a chaotic canvas.

After several wrong turns and a near-collision with a dog walker, he finally found the right building. Taking a deep breath, he walked towards the elevator, the worn brass buttons gleaming under the harsh fluorescent lights. Each floor he ascended seemed to increase his anxiety. Would she like him in her world? Would his small-town charm translate to the fast-paced rhythm of the city?

The elevator doors pinged open, revealing a brightly lit hallway adorned with abstract paintings. Arjun found the apartment number, his hand trembling as he pressed the doorbell. A moment stretched into an eternity before the door swung open.

Riya stood before him, her red hair a beacon in the dimly lit hallway. She wore a simple white t-shirt and jeans, but a radiant smile lit up her face that eclipsed the city lights reflected in her eyes. "Arjun!" she exclaimed, her voice filled with excitement. "You finally made it!"

Before he could respond, she pulled him into a hug, the familiar scent of her vanilla perfume instantly calming his racing heart. He wrapped his arms around her, feeling a sense of belonging he hadn't expected in this concrete jungle.

"Come in, come in," Riya said, ushering him into the apartment. Sunlight streamed through the large windows, illuminating a space that was both artistic and comfortable. Paint tubes and canvases leaned against the walls, a worn armchair sat invitingly by the window, and a bookshelf bulged with art books and novels.

"It's... amazing," Arjun mumbled, taking in the room with a mix of awe and curiosity. It was so different from his own studio, yet it felt... lived in, a reflection of Riya's vibrant personality.

Riya laughed. "It's a bit messy, but it's home," she said, gesturing towards the armchair. "Have a seat, let me take your bags."

As Riya took his backpack, their fingers brushed, sending a jolt of electricity through Arjun. He sank into the armchair, feeling a sense of relief wash over him. He was finally here, with Riya, and that was all that mattered.

Arjun settled deeper into the armchair, the worn leather comforting against his back. He watched Riya move around the room, her movements a graceful dance against the backdrop of the bustling city outside. A faint smile played on his lips as he observed her, a pang of pride welling up within him.

"Would you like some coffee?" Riya asked, setting a mug in front of him and joining him on the floor, leaning against the armchair.

"That would be great," Arjun replied, taking a sip of the warm, comforting beverage. "Black, please."

They lapsed into a comfortable silence, each lost in their own thoughts. Arjun, still getting used to the city's constant hum, watched a couple stroll hand-in-hand through the park below, their figures dwarfed by the towering buildings. Riya, her eyes glued to her phone, scrolled through a newsfeed filled with art exhibitions and upcoming gallery openings.

The silence, while comfortable, wasn't what Arjun had envisioned. He wanted to bridge the gap between their worlds, to understand Riya's life in the city better. He cleared his throat, breaking the quiet.

"So," he began hesitantly, "what's on your agenda for this weekend? Any big art shows you're looking forward to?"

Riya glanced up from her phone, a surprised expression momentarily replacing her usual warmth. "Actually," she admitted, tucking a strand of hair behind her ear, "I haven't planned anything specific. I wanted this weekend to be about us, to show you around the city."

Arjun felt a warmth spread through his chest. "That sounds amazing," he said, a genuine smile replacing his initial nervousness. "But you don't have to cancel your plans for me."

Riya shook her head. "There's always another opening, another critique," she said, her voice soft. "Being here with you, exploring your reaction to the city... that's something I wouldn't trade."

Her words filled him with a newfound confidence. He reached out, his hand hovering hesitantly over hers. "Then maybe," he suggested, a playful glint in his eyes, "I can be your personal guide to the hidden beauty of this concrete jungle."

Riya's lips curved into a smile. "I wouldn't want anyone else," she replied, squeezing his hand gently.

After a moment, Riya stood up, grabbing a worn leather jacket from the back of the chair. "Ready for a city adventure, sunrise artist?" she asked, her voice tinged with excitement.

Arjun chuckled, a spark of anticipation igniting within him. "As ready as I'll ever be," he replied, standing up and taking her hand. He wasn't sure what the city held for him, but with Riya by his side, he was ready to paint his own masterpiece on the urban canvas.

Stepping out of Riya's apartment building, Arjun felt a wave of warmth wash over him despite the cool autumn air. It wasn't just the afternoon sun filtering through the skyscrapers, but the warmth of her presence beside him. Holding her hand, he found the city's cacophony less jarring, almost rhythmic in a way.

Riya, sensing his shift in mood, nudged him playfully. "See? I told you there was hidden beauty even in the concrete jungle."

Arjun grinned. "Maybe you're right," he conceded. "But a guide wouldn't hurt. Where are we headed first?"

Riya glanced around, her eyes twinkling with mischief. "Well, I was thinking..." she trailed off, pointing towards a bustling street lined with colorful food carts. "There's this amazing street vendor who makes the most incredible samosas. They're a must-try, even for a sunrise artist."

Arjun chuckled. Food was definitely one way to explore a new place, and a far cry from his usual breakfast routine of toast and jam. As they navigated the crowded street, the aroma of spices and sizzling meats filled the air, a sensory explosion that both excited and overwhelmed him.

They joined the line at the cart, Riya ordering with practiced ease while Arjun marveled at the vendor's deft hands as he assembled the samosas. The wait was short, filled with Riya's animated descriptions of her favorite city eats and Arjun's shy questions about the local spices.

Finally, they received their steaming samosas, the golden pastry flecked with sesame seeds. Arjun took a tentative bite, a burst of flavor exploding on his tongue. The crisp exterior gave way to a soft, potato filling spiced to perfection. He closed his eyes, savoring the complex mix of textures and tastes.

"See?" Riya said, a triumphant smile on her face. "Told you it was amazing."

Arjun nodded, a wide grin splitting his face. This wasn't just about the food; it was about sharing an experience with Riya, connecting with her world through something as simple and delicious as a street samosa.

Wiping his hands on a napkin, Arjun looked around the bustling street with newfound curiosity. The city, once a daunting landscape, now seemed full of vibrant energy, a symphony of sights, sounds, and smells.

"So," he said, a playful smile on his face, "what else does your city adventure have in store for a small-town boy?"

Riya returned his smile, her eyes sparkling with a secret plan. "Follow me," she said, leading him away from the food carts and down a side street lined with vintage shops and quirky cafes. "Let's explore some hidden gems, sunrise artist. This city may be concrete, but the stories it tells are anything but ordinary."

The afternoon unfolded like a vibrant tapestry, woven with unexpected delights. Riya led Arjun through a labyrinth of narrow streets, each corner revealing a new surprise. They stumbled upon a hidden courtyard filled with sculptures bathed in golden sunlight, a peaceful haven amidst the city's clamor. In a dusty, second-hand bookstore, they unearthed treasures – a first edition poetry collection for Riya and a worn, leather-bound sketchbook for Arjun, perfect for capturing his cityscapes.

At a quaint cafe tucked away in a cobbled alley, they shared steaming mugs of hot chocolate, the rich, dark liquid warming them from the inside out. As they talked, their conversation flowed effortlessly, a mix of comfortable silences and passionate discussions about art, life, and their evolving dreams.

Riya pointed out details Arjun would have missed – the intricate carvings on a weathered doorway, the way the sunlight danced on a stained-glass window, the hidden messages graffiti artists left on brick walls. He saw the city through her eyes, a place teeming with stories waiting to be discovered.

One stop, however, left Arjun speechless. They emerged from a bustling market into a quiet park, a haven of towering trees and manicured gardens. In the center stood a small, open-air gallery, its walls adorned with colorful paintings and sculptures.

Hesitantly, they entered the gallery, greeted by the warm smile of a silver-haired woman behind the counter. Riya introduced them, explaining that Arjun was an artist himself. The woman, who introduced herself as Ms. Chen, invited them to explore the gallery with a twinkle in her eye.

As Arjun walked through the space, his eyes widened in surprise. The artwork displayed wasn't the sleek, conceptual pieces he'd expected from a city gallery. These were vibrant, expressive works that captured the essence of the city's soul – the bustling markets, the towering skyscrapers, the resilience and energy of its people.

He found himself drawn to a particular painting, a kaleidoscope of colors depicting a street vendor selling samosas, their golden pyramids gleaming under the midday sun. A wave of emotions washed over him – the memory of the delicious snack, the thrill of exploring the city with Riya, and the newfound confidence that bloomed within him.

"It's beautiful," Riya whispered, her voice echoing in the quiet space. "It captures the heart of the city, the way you're starting to see it."

Arjun turned to her, a newfound determination stirring within him. "Maybe," he said, his voice filled with newfound purpose, "I can paint the city too. Not just on a canvas, but through the lens you've shown me."

Riya's eyes shone with pride, and a slow smile spread across her face. As the afternoon sun began its descent, casting long shadows across the park, they left the gallery, hand in hand. The city lights were beginning to twinkle on, a promise of a vibrant night ahead.

The day had been an unexpected revelation for Arjun. He hadn't just explored the city; he'd explored a new facet of their connection. He realized Riya wasn't just drawn to his art; she was drawn to the way he saw the world, his ability to capture the beauty in the ordinary. And he, in turn, was falling in love with her city, her passion, and the way she opened his eyes to new possibilities.

As they walked out of the park, the city lights painting the sky in vibrant hues, Arjun knew this weekend was just the beginning. Their story, like a brushstroke on a vast canvas, was waiting to be completed, a masterpiece painted with love, shared experiences, and the vibrant colors of a city that had brought them together.

Chapter 4: A Symphony of Sunrise and City Lights

The city slept in a restless slumber. Streetlights cast an orange glow on empty sidewalks, and the rhythmic hum of traffic had subsided to a low murmur. Arjun lay awake in Riya's guest room, the unfamiliar sounds a lullaby against the backdrop of his racing heart.

He couldn't sleep. The events of the past day replayed in his mind like a kaleidoscope of vibrant images – the unexpected beauty of the hidden courtyard, the delicious warmth of the shared hot chocolate, the awe-inspiring artwork at Ms. Chen's gallery. Most of all, he relived the look in Riya's eyes when he'd spoken of painting the city, a mix of pride and a spark that mirrored his own newfound excitement.

As dawn approached, the faintest blush of pink began to creep across the horizon, painting the edges of the skyscrapers a soft rose. Arjun, unable to contain his anticipation, slipped out of bed and tiptoed towards the window.

The sight that greeted him was unlike any sunrise he'd witnessed before. The golden light filtered through a canvas of glass and steel, reflecting off skyscraper windows and casting long, angular shadows across the streets below. It wasn't the vast expanse of fields he was used to, but it held a unique beauty, a symphony of light and shadow, a dance between nature and human creation.

A sudden warmth on his shoulder startled him. He turned to find Riya standing beside him, a sleepy smile playing on her lips.

"Couldn't sleep either, huh?" she said, her voice a soft murmur.

Arjun shook his head, captivated by the city's awakening. "It's... different," he admitted, searching for the right words. "Beautiful, but different."

Riya leaned closer, her eyes sparkling with amusement. "Different doesn't have to mean bad," she said. "Maybe it just means there's a new kind of sunrise waiting to be captured."

Arjun felt a surge of inspiration course through him. He was right. The city, with its towering buildings and frenetic energy, was a new canvas, a new challenge. He could use his unique perspective, his ability to find beauty in the ordinary, to paint the city in a way it had never been seen before.

"Maybe you're right," he said, a smile spreading across his face. "Maybe it's time I started sketching a city sunrise."

Riya reached out, her hand gently brushing his. "I'd love to see that," she said, her voice filled with warmth. "But before that, how about some coffee? We can plan your city sunrise masterpiece fueled by caffeine."

The thought of capturing the city's awakening on canvas filled him with a thrilling anticipation. He turned to Riya, her eyes shining with the same excitement he felt. In that moment, he knew this wasn't just about painting a sunrise; it was about capturing a new beginning, a shared journey on a canvas far larger than any they'd ever imagined.

The aroma of freshly brewed coffee filled the air as Riya and Arjun sat at the kitchen table, bathed in the soft glow of the morning sun. Steam swirled from their mugs, mingling with the excitement brewing within them.

"So, sunrise artist," Riya said, a playful glint in her eyes. "Where do you see your first city masterpiece taking place?"

Arjun tapped his chin thoughtfully, his gaze flitting across the cityscape visible through the window. "There's something about that rooftop across the street," he mused, pointing towards a building with a flat, accessible roof. "It offers a panoramic view of the city, a perfect place to capture the sunrise playing across the different heights of the buildings."

Riya's eyes widened. "The Thompson building? That roof is usually off-limits, even for residents. It's for maintenance access only."

Arjun's smile faltered slightly. The idea of sneaking onto a rooftop for the perfect shot wasn't exactly his usual artistic process, but the image in his mind was too compelling to abandon. "Maybe we can talk to the building manager?" he suggested, a hint of hope in his voice.

Riya shook her head, a mischievous grin replacing her concern. "There's a better way," she declared, her voice dropping to a conspiratorial whisper. "My friend Maya lives in that building. She's an artist too, and a bit of a rebel with a cause. If anyone can get us access, it's her."

A surge of relief washed over Arjun. He wasn't sure about the "rebel" part, but Maya sounded like their best chance. The prospect of meeting another artist, especially one who might understand his artistic vision, added another layer of excitement to the morning.

"Sounds perfect," he agreed, a smile mirroring Riya's. "Let's call her then. The sooner we secure that rooftop, the sooner I can capture this city sunrise symphony."

As Riya dialed Maya's number, a sense of anticipation buzzed through the air. This wasn't just about painting a sunrise; it was about pushing boundaries, exploring the city together, and creating a shared experience that would forever be etched in their memories.

The dial tone hummed impatiently in Riya's ear as Maya's phone rang. Arjun watched her, his nerves growing with each unanswered ring. Just as he was about to suggest another option, Riya's face lit up.

"Maya!" she exclaimed, a wide grin spreading across her face. "Listen, I have a favor to ask..."

Riya's voice filled the room as she explained their predicament and Arjun's artistic vision. He listened intently, catching glimpses of amusement and surprise in her expressions as she relayed Maya's reactions. Finally, Riya hung up the phone, a triumphant glint in her eyes.

"We're in," she announced, throwing her arms around Arjun in a spontaneous hug. "Maya's a kindred spirit, just like I thought. She loves your idea and is all for a secret rooftop sunrise adventure."

Arjun squeezed her back, a wave of relief and excitement washing over him. He couldn't believe their plan was actually coming together. "That's amazing!" he exclaimed. "But how do we get up there?"

Riya winked. "Leave that to Maya," she said mysteriously. "She has her ways. Just be ready for a little... unconventional access."

The next few hours flew by in a flurry of activity. Arjun prepped his paints and brushes, his excitement mounting with each dab of color on his palette. Riya packed a backpack with essentials – water, snacks, a first-aid kit (just in case), and most importantly, a camera to capture their rooftop escapade.

Finally, just as the sun began its descent towards the horizon, casting long shadows across the city, Riya received a text from Maya. "Operation Sunrise is a go," it read, followed by a series of emojis that hinted at mischief.

With a mix of trepidation and excitement, they hailed a cab and headed towards the Thompson building. The closer they got, the more imposing it seemed, a steel and glass giant amidst the bustling city streets. Arjun couldn't help but wonder what unconventional access Maya had in mind.

The Thompson building loomed large as they stepped out of the cab, its sleek facade reflecting the city lights in a thousand shimmering fragments. Compared to its imposing stature, Arjun felt small, a mere speck against the urban jungle. His initial excitement was tinged with a nervous tremor as he glanced at Riya, seeking reassurance.

Riya, however, exuded an air of casual confidence. "Ready for a little artistic rebellion?" she asked, a playful glint in her eyes.

Arjun managed a shaky smile. "As ready as I'll ever be for a rooftop adventure on a whim," he replied, his voice betraying his apprehension.

Riya laughed, the sound echoing reassuringly in the quiet street. "Don't worry," she said, squeezing his hand. "Maya knows what she's doing."

Following Riya's lead, they entered the building's brightly lit lobby, a stark contrast to the fading light outside. While Riya distracted the doorman with a well-rehearsed story about visiting a friend who had "accidentally" locked themselves out, Arjun scanned the surroundings, searching for any sign of Maya.

Suddenly, a flash of movement caught his eye. A young woman with a shock of blue hair peeked out from behind a large potted plant, a mischievous grin plastered on her face. This, he presumed, was Maya.

"There you are!" Riya whispered, ushering Arjun closer. "Maya, this is Arjun. Arjun, meet the mastermind behind our rooftop escapade."

Maya extended a hand, her smile even wider. "Nice to meet you, sunrise artist," she said in a voice surprisingly calm for someone about to help them commit a minor act of trespassing. "Don't worry, I have a secret passage that leads straight to the roof. It's a little dusty, but perfectly safe."

Intrigued, Arjun followed Maya and Riya through a maze of dimly lit hallways and back corridors. They navigated a labyrinth of storage rooms stacked with cleaning supplies and forgotten furniture, the air thick with the musty scent of disuse.

Finally, Maya stopped in front of a nondescript metal door, its worn paint barely clinging to the surface. With a flourish, she retrieved a key ring from her pocket, the keys jangling like a mischievous symphony.

"This," she declared, inserting a small, rusty key into the lock, "is the gateway to our artistic sanctuary."

With a satisfying click, the door creaked open, revealing a narrow, rickety staircase spiraling upwards. A single bare bulb cast flickering shadows on the dusty steps, adding an element of intrigue and a hint of danger to their adventure.

Arjun hesitated, his apprehension returning. "Are you sure this is safe?" he asked, his voice barely a whisper.

Maya winked. "Safe? Maybe not exactly," she admitted, a devil-may-care attitude radiating from her. "But definitely exciting. Come on, the sunrise won't wait forever!"

Taking a deep breath, Arjun decided to embrace the unconventional. With Riya close behind, he followed Maya up the rickety stairs, the uneven steps creaking under their weight. The air grew colder and thinner as they ascended, a stark contrast to the warmth within the building.

The climb seemed endless, each turn revealing another dusty step and another flicker of doubt in Arjun's mind. But then, with a final groan and a burst of light, they emerged onto a small, flat rooftop.

The sight that greeted them was breathtaking. The sprawling cityscape stretched out before them, a canvas bathed in the golden hues of the setting sun. The buildings, once imposing giants, now transformed into majestic silhouettes, their glass windows reflecting the fading light in a million shimmering prisms. In the distance, the city lights were beginning to twinkle on like a scattering of stars.

Arjun stood frozen, mesmerized by the sight. It was a cityscape he'd never witnessed before – a symphony of light and shadow, a dance between nature and human creation. The city, once daunting, now captivated him with its frenetic energy and undeniable beauty.

Riya gasped beside him, her eyes mirroring the awe in his own. "It's... perfect," she breathed, her voice filled with wonder.

Maya grinned, a hint of pride in her eyes. "Told you it was a secret worth sharing," she said, pulling out a worn blanket from her backpack. "Now, before we get lost in the view, let's get comfortable. The show's about to begin."

They settled down on the blanket, their backs against the low parapet wall, the cool night air brushing against their faces. As the last sliver of sun dipped below the horizon, painting the sky in a vibrant palette of orange, pink,

Chapter 5: Colors of a New Dawn

The city lights, like a billion fireflies awakening, began to weave their magic into the twilight canvas. The fiery hues of the sunset softened into a gentle lavender, and a crescent moon peeked through the inky blackness, casting a silvery glow on the buildings below. Arjun, still mesmerized by the panorama before him, felt a wave of inspiration wash over him. He reached for his backpack, his fingers brushing against the worn leather of his sketchbook.

"Ready to capture this city symphony, sunrise artist?" Riya asked, her voice a soft whisper in the cool night air.

Arjun looked at her, the city lights reflected in her eyes. "More than ever," he replied, a newfound confidence blooming in his chest. This wasn't just about painting a sunrise; it was about capturing a new beginning, a shared experience on a canvas far larger than anything he'd ever imagined.

He uncapped his pen, the scratch of nib on paper resonating with the quiet hum of the city below. He started with quick, loose strokes, trying to capture the essence of the cityscape — the towering buildings, the twinkling lights, the relentless energy that pulsed through the urban arteries.

But something felt missing. The sketch, though technically sound, lacked the soul of the city, the feeling that had captivated him. He paused, frustration gnawing at him. He glanced at Riya, hoping to find a spark of inspiration in her eyes.

Riya, as if sensing his struggle, leaned closer, her hand brushing against his. "What's wrong?" she asked, her voice laced with concern.

"I can't seem to capture it," Arjun confessed, gesturing towards the city lights. "The sketch feels... lifeless."

Riya smiled, a knowing glint in her eyes. "Maybe you're looking at the city the wrong way," she suggested. "It's not just steel and glass, Arjun. It's a living, breathing entity – a canvas of stories waiting to be told."

Her words resonated with him. He closed his eyes for a moment, trying to see the city through her eyes. He imagined the people in the buildings below, their lives unfolding like tiny dramas against the backdrop of the city lights. He pictured the artists in their studios, pouring their souls onto canvases. He heard the rhythmic hum of traffic, not as noise, but as a symphony of purposeful movement.

When he opened his eyes again, the cityscape seemed different. He saw the beauty not just in the architecture, but in the stories it held. He saw the vibrant energy of the city, the relentless spirit that never slept.

He picked up his pen once more, this time with renewed purpose. His strokes became more deliberate, capturing the essence of the city's soul. He used vibrant colors to represent the energy, muted tones for the quiet moments, and swirling lines to depict the constant movement. He sketched the details – a lone taxi cab weaving through traffic, a couple sharing a romantic kiss on a rooftop bar, a window glowing with the warm light of a home.

With each stroke, the city on his canvas came alive. It was no longer a static landscape, but a vibrant tapestry of stories, emotions, and experiences. He felt a deep satisfaction course through him, a sense of accomplishment he hadn't felt in a long time.

He looked at Riya, eager to share his creation. "What do you think?" he asked, holding up the sketchbook.

Riya's eyes widened in surprise, a smile blossoming on her face. "Wow, Arjun," she breathed. "It's... it's incredible. You captured the heart of the city, the energy, the stories."

Arjun felt a warmth spread through him, a validation of his artistic vision. This wasn't just a painting; it was a bridge between his world and Riya's. It was a way for him to express the newfound love he felt for the city, a love that began with her.

"You helped me see it," he admitted, his voice filled with gratitude. "You showed me the city through your eyes, and it changed the way I see it forever."

Riya leaned closer, her eyes sparkling with affection. "It's not just the city you see differently," she whispered. "Maybe it's also us."

Arjun returned her gaze, a new understanding dawning on him. This experience, this shared adventure, had brought them closer, their connection deepening with each brushstroke, each shared sunrise and city light. They had embarked on this journey as two artists, but they were leaving as something more.

A gentle breeze swept across the rooftop, carrying the faint sounds of the city – laughter from a rooftop party, the strumming of a guitar from an open window, the quiet rumble

A gentle breeze swept across the rooftop, carrying the faint sounds of the city – laughter from a rooftop party, the strumming of a guitar from an open window, the quiet rumble of a passing train. The symphony of the city, once overwhelming, now felt like a comforting lullaby.

Arjun leaned back against the parapet wall, his gaze lingering on Riya's face. The city lights cast an ethereal glow upon her, highlighting the soft curve of her cheekbones and the sparkle in her eyes. He felt a sense of belonging he hadn't expected, a connection that transcended the boundaries of their different worlds.

"This isn't how I imagined spending our weekend," Riya admitted, a playful smile gracing her lips.

"Me neither," Arjun chuckled, "but I wouldn't trade it for anything."

A comfortable silence settled between them, punctuated only by the sounds of the city and the occasional rustle of turning pages in Arjun's sketchbook. As the hours melted into the early morning, the sky began to lighten, revealing the first streaks of dawn. A blush of pink crept across the horizon, painting the edges of the buildings in a soft, ethereal glow.

Arjun watched, mesmerized, as the city slowly awakened. Lights flickered off in apartment buildings, replaced by the warm glow of lamps as people began their day. Traffic started picking up, weaving a network of amber brake lights across the city arteries. The symphony of the city shifted, the gentle hum of the night replaced by the steady thrum of a bustling new day.

Suddenly, inspiration struck him. With a newfound urgency, he grabbed his paints and brushes. He squeezed out vibrant hues of pink, orange, and gold onto his palette, eager to capture the nascent dawn on his canvas.

"The city's waking up," Riya observed, her voice filled with wonder.

Arjun nodded, his brushstrokes becoming more rapid, capturing the fleeting beauty of the dawn light. He painted the way the pink hues danced across the glass facades, the way the skyscrapers cast long shadows across the streets below. He added a splash of red to depict the taillights of a passing fire truck, a reminder of the city's constant pulse.

As he worked, a sense of peace settled over him. The initial apprehension about the rooftop adventure had melted away, replaced by a sense of accomplishment and a newfound appreciation for the city's energy. He had captured not just a sunrise, but a moment in time, a shared experience that would forever be etched in his memory.

Finally, with a satisfied sigh, he stepped back from his easel. The canvas vibrated with color and light, a testament to the beauty he had discovered in the heart of the concrete jungle.

"Wow," Riya breathed, her eyes wide with appreciation. "It's breathtaking, Arjun. You captured the city's awakening, the promise of a new day."

Arjun smiled, warmth spreading through him. "It's not just the city," he said, his voice filled with emotion. "It's also us. This weekend, this experience, it's a new beginning for us, isn't it?"

Riya met his gaze, her eyes reflecting the same sentiment. A slow, genuine smile spread across her face. "Yes," she whispered, her voice barely audible over the morning sounds. "It's a new dawn, for the city, for us, and for our art."

In that quiet moment, bathed in the soft light of the rising sun, they stood hand in hand, their connection solidified not just by words, but by a shared experience and the vibrant colors of a city sunrise that had painted their future with a new and exciting palette.

The city stretched out before them, a canvas of possibilities waiting to be explored. The initial fear and apprehension of the city, for Arjun, had transformed into a deep respect and a desire to capture its essence in his art. Riya, in turn, saw her city anew, not just through her own eyes, but through the lens of his artistic vision.

As the sun climbed higher in the sky, casting its golden light across the urban landscape, they knew this was just the beginning of their journey. They were no longer just two artists from different worlds; they were partners, collaborators, ready to paint their own masterpiece on the vast canvas of life, a masterpiece infused with the vibrant colors of love, shared experiences, and the magic of a city that had brought them together.

The first rays of sunlight glinted off the paint on their palettes, a promise of new beginnings, new artistic endeavors, and a love story that, like the city itself, was forever in motion, vibrant, and ever-evolving.

The descent back to reality was swift and almost jarring. Emerging from the building's back exit, they were greeted by the bustling morning rush hour. Cars honked, pedestrians hurried with purposeful strides, and the air thrummed with the city's relentless energy.

Arjun felt a slight pang of nostalgia for the quiet peace of the rooftop, but it was quickly replaced by a thrill of anticipation. They had a story to share, an adventure to recount, and a future to chart together.

"So," Riya began, a playful glint in her eyes as they walked towards her apartment, "how do you convince a building manager to grant access to a rooftop for an impromptu sunrise art session?"

Arjun chuckled. "Maybe a little creative persuasion, in the form of a painting?" he suggested, glancing at the vibrant canvas tucked under his arm.

Riya's eyes widened. "You'd do that?"

"Absolutely," Arjun replied with a confident smile. "Consider it a peace offering for our little rooftop escapade."

They reached Riya's apartment building, and as they ascended the stairs, Arjun couldn't help but notice a newfound lightness in her step. The city, once a canvas of unfamiliar sights and sounds, now held a sense of comfort and familiarity. He had seen it through her eyes, and in the process, fallen in love not just with her, but with the pulsating heart of the city itself.

Back in the apartment, Riya brewed a fresh pot of coffee, the aroma filling the air and chasing away any lingering drowsiness. Arjun spread out his sunrise painting on the living room table, the vibrant colors a stark contrast against the neutral tones of the room.

A knock on the door startled them. Riya exchanged a surprised glance with Arjun before heading to answer it. A moment later, she was back, ushering in a man with a confused expression.

"Arjun, this is Mr. Patel, the building manager," Riya explained, her voice laced with a hint of nervousness.

Mr. Patel eyed Arjun and the painting with suspicion. "Yes?" he asked curtly.

"Mr. Patel," Arjun began, extending his hand in greeting. "I apologize for any inconvenience caused by our... unconventional access to the rooftop."

Mr. Patel's lips pursed further, and Arjun felt a wave of apprehension. He was about to apologize again when Riya stepped forward.

"Actually, Mr. Patel," she interjected, a mischievous glint in her eyes, "Arjun might have a proposition for you."

She gestured towards the painting, and Mr. Patel's gaze flitted towards it, curiosity softening his previously stern expression. He approached the table, his eyes narrowing as he examined the cityscape bathed in the golden hues of dawn.

A moment of silence stretched between them as Mr. Patel studied the painting. Then, to Arjun's surprise, a slow smile spread across his face.

"Interesting," he remarked, his voice gruff but laced with a hint of admiration. "You've captured the city in a way I've never seen before."

Arjun felt a surge of relief wash over him. "Thank you," he replied, his voice filled with gratitude.

Mr. Patel continued to study the painting, a thoughtful expression etched on his face. Finally, he looked up at Arjun.

"Tell you what," he said, a twinkle in his eye. "You make a donation of this painting to the building's new community center, and we'll call it even."

Arjun and Riya exchanged a surprised look. This wasn't what they expected, but it was certainly an unexpected turn of events.

"Are you serious?" Arjun asked, blinking in disbelief.

Mr. Patel chuckled. "Serious as a heart attack, son. This painting belongs in this building, a reminder of the beauty that exists even in the heart of the concrete jungle."

Arjun couldn't help but smile. This was an even better outcome than he could have hoped for. His painting, a product of this shared adventure with Riya, would find a permanent home, a constant reminder of the city and the love story that blossomed within its vibrant chaos.

"I'd be honored," he replied, extending his hand towards Mr. Patel.

Mr. Patel shook his hand firmly, a newfound respect shining in his eyes. "Welcome to the city, son," he said, a hint of warmth in his voice. "You might just find it grows on you."

Arjun returned his smile, a sense of belonging blooming in his chest. The city, once a daunting labyrinth, now felt like a canvas waiting to be further explored, a canvas he would explore hand-in-hand with the woman who had shown him

As the days turned into weeks, Arjun's initial apprehension about the city life melted away completely. He found himself drawn to its bustling streets, its hidden alleyways, and the cacophony of sounds that once overwhelmed him now felt like a soothing symphony. He explored the city with newfound enthusiasm, each corner revealing a new story waiting to be captured on his canvas.

Riya became his guide and muse, leading him to bustling art markets, hidden rooftop cafes with breathtaking views, and quiet parks where artists gathered to sketch and share ideas. They spent their evenings discussing their art, their dreams, and their shared love for this ever-evolving city.

Arjun's painting of the city sunrise, now proudly displayed in the building's community center, became a talking point. It sparked conversations about appreciating urban beauty, the power of art, and the unexpected connections that could be forged in the heart of a concrete jungle. Local artists approached Arjun, impressed by his unique perspective, and soon he found himself part of a vibrant artistic community, sharing his skills and learning from others.

One evening, as they sat on their rooftop haven, watching the city lights paint the night sky, Riya rested her head on Arjun's shoulder. "Remember our first city sunrise?" she asked, her voice laced with a hint of nostalgia.

Arjun smiled, the memory vivid in his mind. "How could I forget? Sneaking onto a rooftop, chasing the sunrise, and getting a building manager to accept a painting as an apology."

Riya laughed, a sound that echoed across the rooftop. "It was more than an apology," she said. "It was the beginning of our city adventure, our artistic partnership."

Arjun took her hand in his, his fingers intertwining with hers. "An adventure that changed everything," he whispered, his gaze fixed on the glittering cityscape. "It showed me a new side of the city, and it showed me the woman I never knew I was looking for."

Riya turned to him, her eyes reflecting the city lights. "And you showed me the beauty of a world beyond my own, the power of seeing things through different eyes."

They sat in comfortable silence, the city lights twinkling around them like promises whispered in the night. The future stretched before them, a vast canvas filled with possibilities. They knew their journey had just begun, a journey of artistic exploration, shared experiences, and a love story that thrived in the vibrant rhythm of their adopted city. The city that had brought them together, with its relentless energy and hidden beauty, would forever be a part of their story, a constant reminder of the magic that bloomed under the golden hues of a city sunrise.

Conclusion

The last rays of the setting sun dipped below the horizon, painting the cityscape in a palette of fiery orange and deep purple. Arjun and Riya stood on their rooftop haven, their silhouettes etched against the vibrant canvas. It had been a year since their sunrise escapade, a year filled with artistic exploration, deepening love, and the exhilarating embrace of city life.

Arjun looked at Riya, the city lights reflected in her eyes. She was no longer just his muse; she was his partner, his confidante, his home in this concrete jungle. Together, they had navigated the city's labyrinthine streets, discovered hidden gems, and created art that resonated with the urban soul.

A cool breeze ruffled their hair, carrying the sounds of the city – the wail of distant sirens, the rhythmic hum of traffic, the laughter of children playing in a nearby park. It was a symphony that once overwhelmed him, but now felt like a comforting lullaby, a constant reminder of the city's vibrant heartbeat.

He looked back at his latest painting, a vibrant depiction of a bustling street market, teeming with life and color. It was a tribute to the city's energy, its diversity, and the stories that unfolded on its streets every single day.

Riya squeezed his hand, her touch grounding him in the present. "Ready for tomorrow's gallery opening?" she asked, a hint of nervous excitement in her voice.

Arjun smiled, a thrill coursing through him. Their first joint exhibition, featuring works inspired by their city adventure, was a testament to their artistic partnership and their love for the city that had brought them together.

"More than ready," he replied, his gaze meeting hers. "We've come a long way, haven't we?"

Riya returned his smile, her eyes sparkling with pride. "From rooftop rebels to celebrated artists," she teased, "we've definitely made our mark on the city."

They leaned closer, their laughter echoing across the rooftop. The future stretched before them, a vast canvas filled with possibilities. They knew their journey had just begun, a journey of artistic exploration, shared dreams, and a love story that thrived under the neon glow of their adopted city. The city that had brought them together, with its relentless energy and hidden beauty, would forever be a part of their story, a constant reminder of the magic that bloomed under the golden hues of a city sunrise.

As they turned back to the city, their hands intertwined, they walked hand-in-hand towards their future, ready to paint their own masterpiece on the vast canvas of life, a masterpiece infused with the vibrant colors of their love and the city that had become their home.

About the Author

Mrigendra Bharti, born on June 29, 2004, in South Delhi, India, is a multifaceted individual recognized as the owner of Mrigendra Bharti Group InfoTech India Co. Pvt Ltd. Beyond his entrepreneurial endeavors, he is a distinguished music producer, director, and a budding writer.

Embarking on his professional journey at a young age, Mrigendra Bharti's visionary leadership has led to the establishment of several successful ventures, including Croma Music Series Entertainment, Sellbrochure, Fauget Innovative, and more.

What sets Mrigendra apart is his early initiation into the world of business. His foray into the unknown realms of entrepreneurship began during his 10th-grade years, where he delved into the music industry. This initial venture laid the foundation for subsequent achievements, showcasing his dedication and resilience.

Having honed his skills in music, Mrigendra Bharti not only demonstrated significant growth in his craft but also expanded his professional network. His passion extends beyond music, encompassing app and website development, as well as graphic design.

Fueled by his creative aspirations, Mrigendra established the Mrigendra Bharti Group, a company specializing in website and app development. Currently, he collaborates with a dedicated team, collectively working on ambitious projects that promise innovation and excellence.

Mrigendra's journey serves as an inspiration, particularly for today's students, highlighting the potential of youthful determination and the ability to transform innovative ideas into successful businesses. As he continues to make strides in various domains, Mrigendra Bharti remains a dynamic force, contributing vibrancy to the realms of business, music, and technology.

Read more at https://www.imwriter-mrigendra.rf.gd.

www.ingramcontent.com/pod-product-compliance
Lightning Source LLC
Chambersburg PA
CBHW052127150726
48002CB00006B/2512